SABAN'S

MIGHTY MORPHIN POWER RANGERS

2

WRITTEN BY
KYLE HIGGINS
ILLUSTRATED BY
HENDRY PRASETYA

COLORS BY
MATT HERMS
LETTERS BY
ED DUKESHIRE

COVER BY
JAMAL CAMPBELL
DESIGNER
JILLIAN CRAB
ASSISTANT EDITOR
ALEX GALER
EDITOR
DAFNA PLEBAN

HASBRO SPECIAL THANKS
BRIAN CASENTINI,
MELISSA FLORES,
EDGAR PASTEN,
PAUL STRICKLAND,
MARCY GEORGE,
JASON BISCHOFF,
ED LANE,
BETH ARTALE,
AND **MICHAEL KELLY**

ABDO Spotlight
BOOM! STUDIOS
Licensed by: Hasbro

ABDOBOOKS.COM

Reinforced library bound edition published in 2020 by Spotlight, a division of ABDO, PO Box 398166, Minneapolis, Minnesota 55439. Spotlight produces high-quality reinforced library bound editions for schools and libraries. Published by agreement with BOOM! Studios.

Printed in the United States of America, North Mankato, Minnesota.
092019
012020

THIS BOOK CONTAINS RECYCLED MATERIALS

Licensed by:

Library of Congress Control Number: 2019942386

Publisher's Cataloging-in-Publication Data

Names: Higgins, Kyle, author. | Prasetya, Hendry; Herms, Matt; Silas, Thony; Valenza, Bryan; illustrators.
Title: Mighty morphin power rangers/ writer: Kyle Higgins; art: Hendry Prasetya; Matt Herms; Thony Silas; Bryan Valenza.
Description: Minneapolis, Minnesota: Spotlight, 2020 | Series: Mighty morphin power rangers
Summary: Tommy Oliver was new in town when evil doer, Rita Repulsa, made him the Green Ranger. After escaping her mind control, he hopes for a normal life, which isn't easy to do with the plights of high school, making new friends, and the dangers that come with being a Power Ranger.
Identifiers: ISBN 9781532144233 (#1, lib. bdg.) | ISBN 9781532144240 (#2, lib. bdg.) | ISBN 9781532144257 (#3, lib. bdg.) | ISBN 9781532144264 (#4, lib. bdg.) | ISBN 9781532144271 (#5, lib. bdg.) | ISBN 9781532144288 (#6, lib. bdg.) | ISBN 9781532144295 (#7, lib. bdg.) | ISBN 9781532144301 (#8, lib. bdg.) | ISBN 9781532144318 (#9, lib. bdg.)
Subjects: LCSH: Mighty Morphin Power Rangers (Television program)--Juvenile fiction. | Ninjas--Juvenile fiction. | Superheroes--Juvenile fiction. | Good and evil--Juvenile fiction. | Graphic novels--Juvenile fiction. | Comic books, strips, etc.--Juvenile fiction
Classification: DDC 741.5--dc23

Spotlight

A Division of ABDO
abdobooks.com

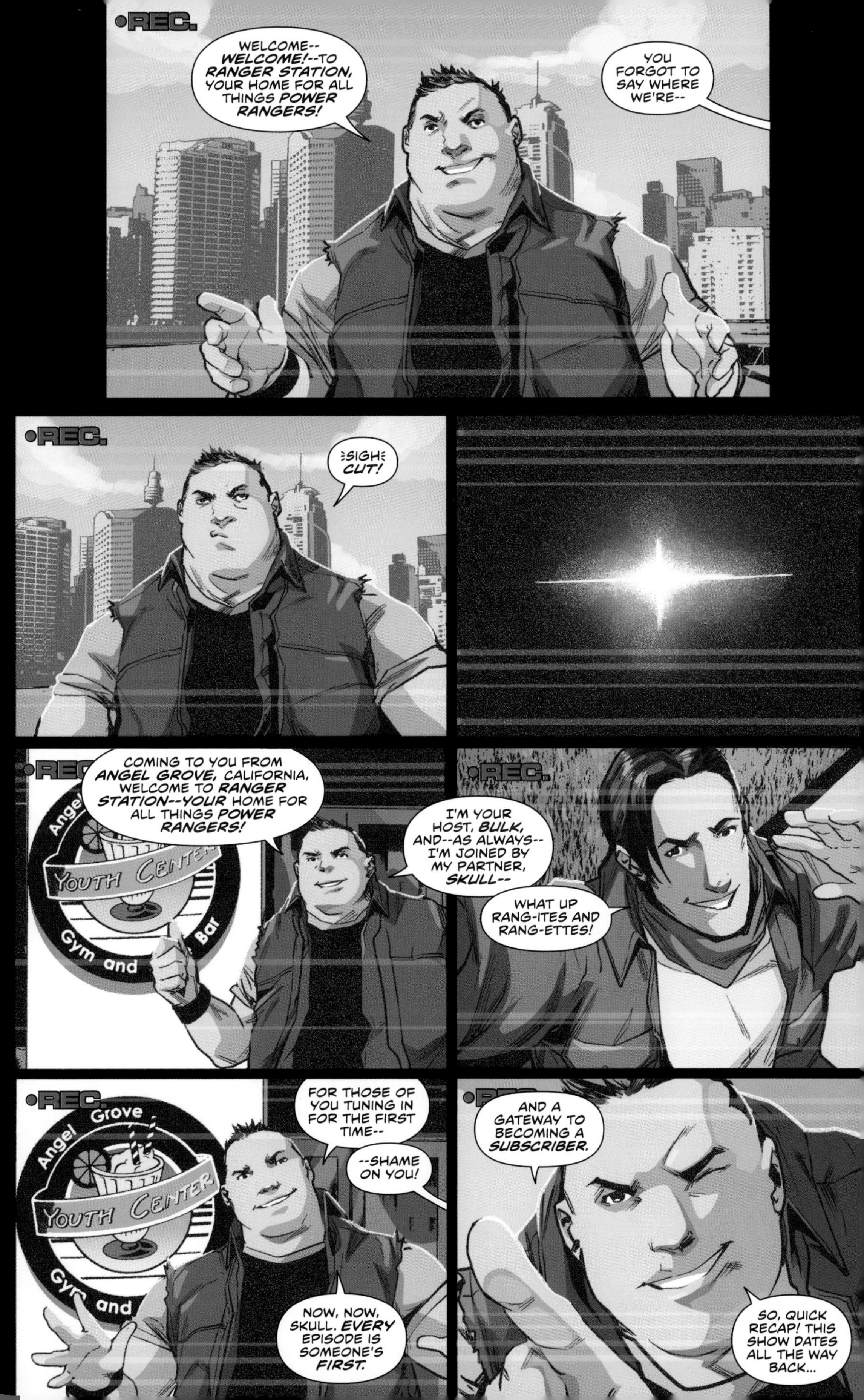
REC.
WELCOME--WELCOME!--TO RANGER STATION, YOUR HOME FOR ALL THINGS POWER RANGERS!
YOU FORGOT TO SAY WHERE WE'RE--
REC.
SIGH CUT!
REC.
COMING TO YOU FROM ANGEL GROVE, CALIFORNIA, WELCOME TO RANGER STATION--YOUR HOME FOR ALL THINGS POWER RANGERS!
Angel
YOUTH CENTER
Gym and
Bar
REC.
I'M YOUR HOST, BULK, AND--AS ALWAYS--I'M JOINED BY MY PARTNER, SKULL--
WHAT UP RANG-ITES AND RANG-ETTES!
REC.
Angel Grove
YOUTH CENTER
Gym and
FOR THOSE OF YOU TUNING IN FOR THE FIRST TIME--
--SHAME ON YOU!
NOW, NOW, SKULL. EVERY EPISODE IS SOMEONE'S FIRST.
AND A GATEWAY TO BECOMING A SUBSCRIBER.
SO, QUICK RECAP! THIS SHOW DATES ALL THE WAY BACK...

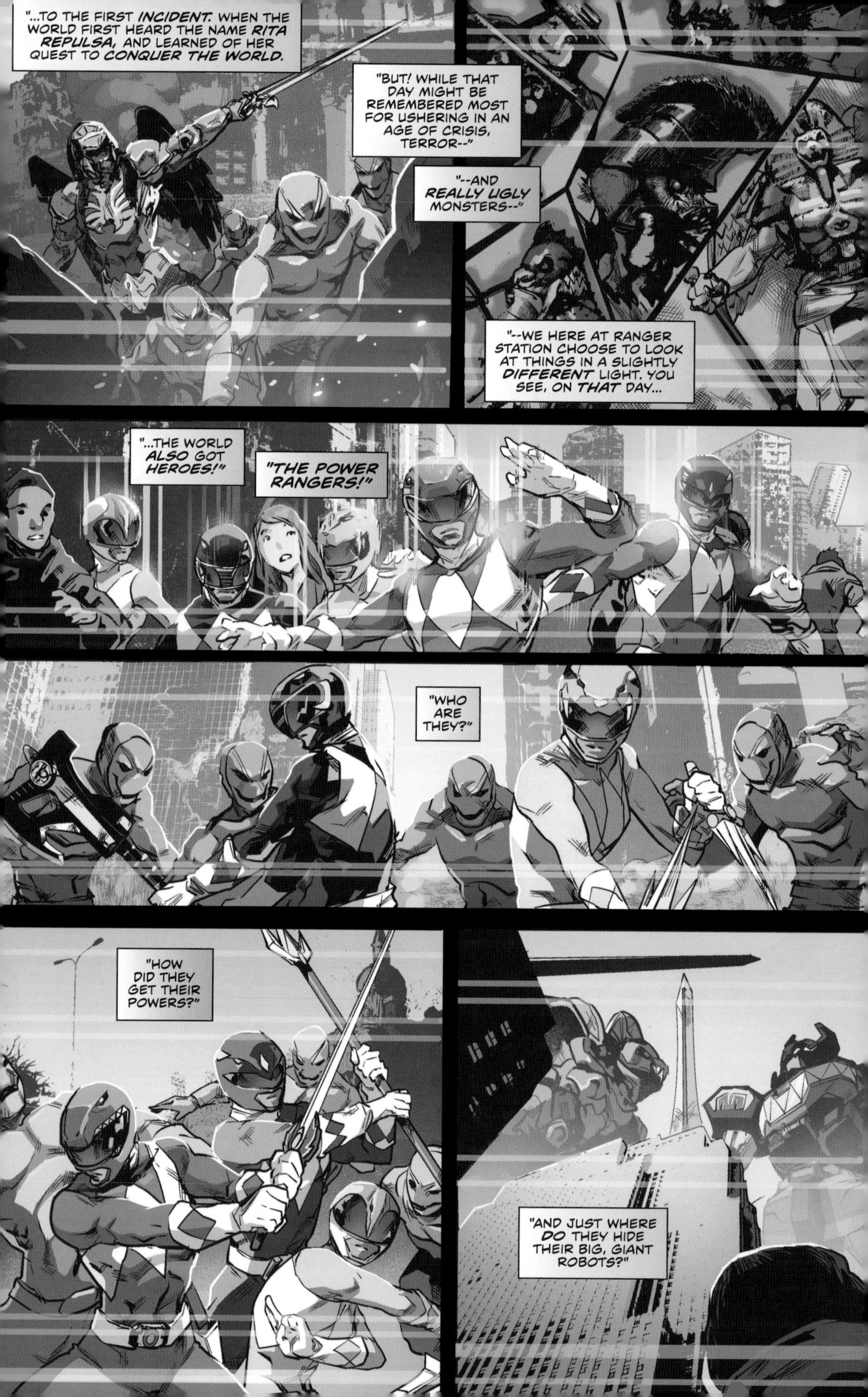
"...TO THE FIRST INCIDENT. WHEN THE WORLD FIRST HEARD THE NAME RITA REPULSA, AND LEARNED OF HER QUEST TO CONQUER THE WORLD.
"BUT! WHILE THAT DAY MIGHT BE REMEMBERED MOST FOR USHERING IN AN AGE OF CRISIS, TERROR--"
"--AND REALLY UGLY MONSTERS--"
"--WE HERE AT RANGER STATION CHOOSE TO LOOK AT THINGS IN A SLIGHTLY DIFFERENT LIGHT. YOU SEE, ON THAT DAY...
"...THE WORLD ALSO GOT HEROES!"
"THE POWER RANGERS!"
"WHO ARE THEY?"
"HOW DID THEY GET THEIR POWERS?"
"AND JUST WHERE DO THEY HIDE THEIR BIG, GIANT ROBOTS?"

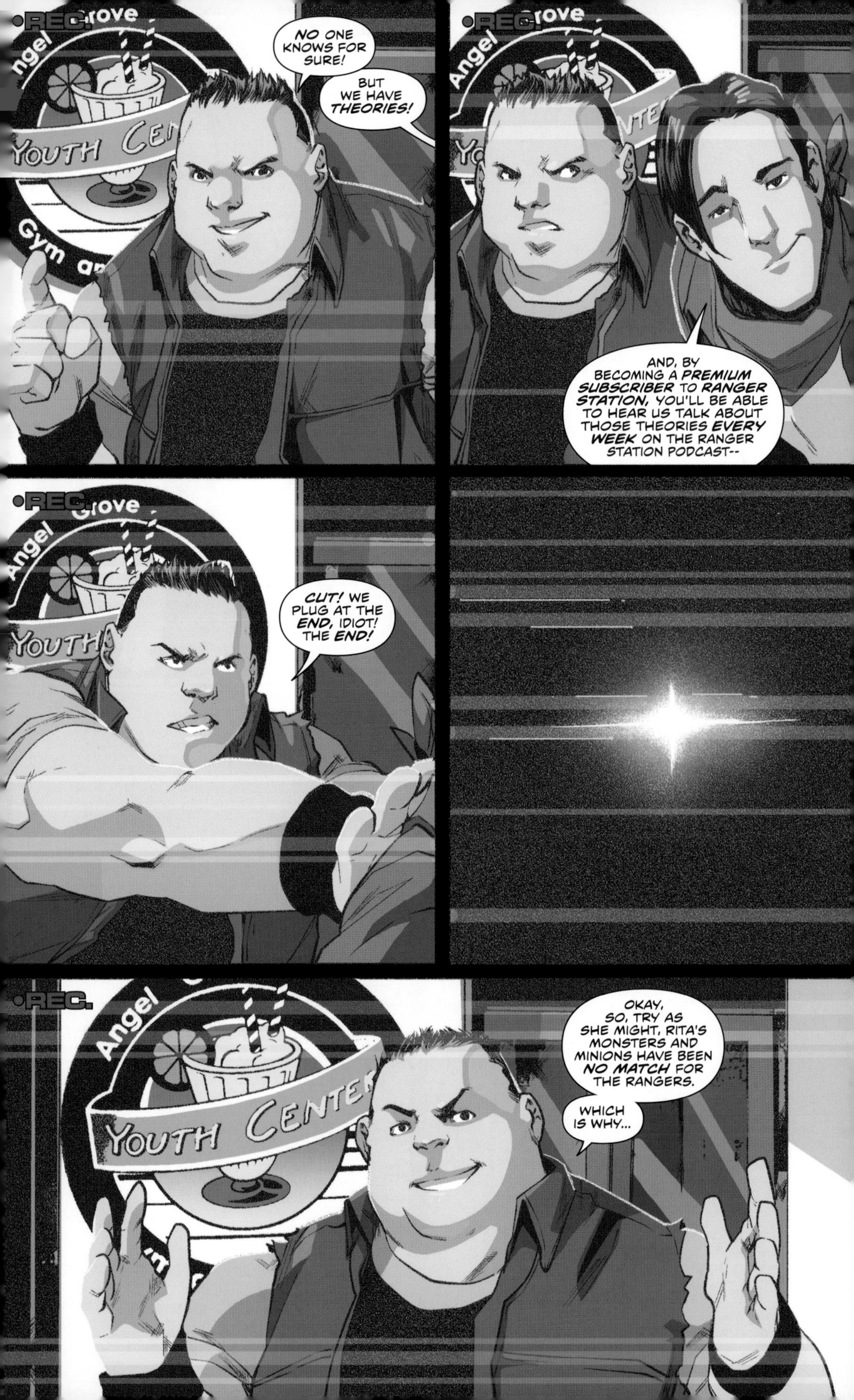

•REC.
Angel Grove
YOUTH CEN
Gym an
NO ONE KNOWS FOR SURE!
BUT WE HAVE THEORIES!
•REC.
AND, BY BECOMING A PREMIUM SUBSCRIBER TO RANGER STATION, YOU'LL BE ABLE TO HEAR US TALK ABOUT THOSE THEORIES EVERY WEEK ON THE RANGER STATION PODCAST--
•REC.
CUT! WE PLUG AT THE END, IDIOT! THE END!
•REC.
Angel
YOUTH CENTER
OKAY, SO, TRY AS SHE MIGHT, RITA'S MONSTERS AND MINIONS HAVE BEEN NO MATCH FOR THE RANGERS.
WHICH IS WHY...

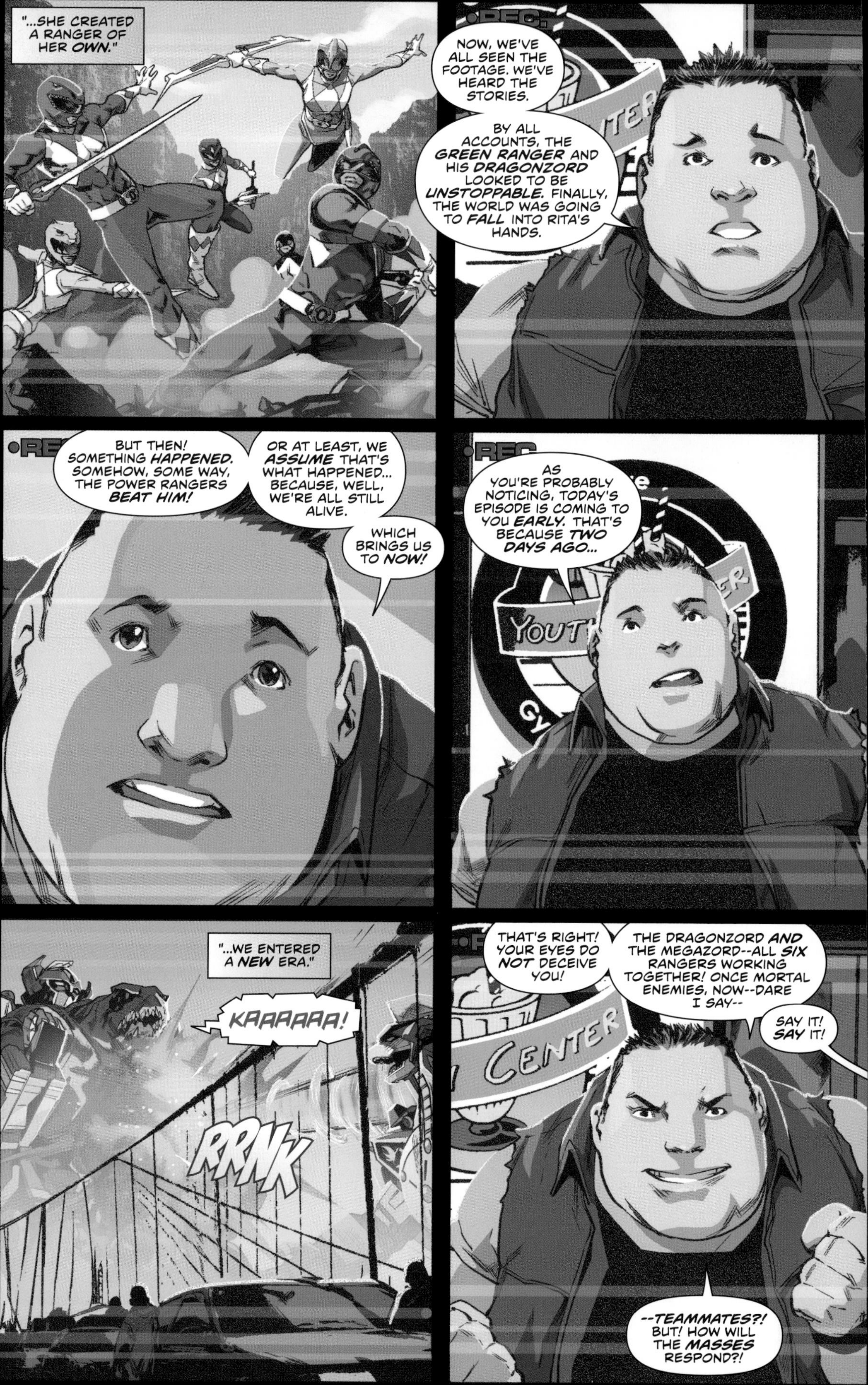
"...SHE CREATED A RANGER OF HER OWN."
REC
NOW, WE'VE ALL SEEN THE FOOTAGE. WE'VE HEARD THE STORIES.
BY ALL ACCOUNTS, THE GREEN RANGER AND HIS DRAGONZORD LOOKED TO BE UNSTOPPABLE. FINALLY, THE WORLD WAS GOING TO FALL INTO RITA'S HANDS.
BUT THEN! SOMETHING HAPPENED. SOMEHOW, SOME WAY, THE POWER RANGERS BEAT HIM!
OR AT LEAST, WE ASSUME THAT'S WHAT HAPPENED... BECAUSE, WELL, WE'RE ALL STILL ALIVE.
WHICH BRINGS US TO NOW!
REC
AS YOU'RE PROBABLY NOTICING, TODAY'S EPISODE IS COMING TO YOU EARLY. THAT'S BECAUSE TWO DAYS AGO...
"...WE ENTERED A NEW ERA."
KAAAAAA!
RRNK
THAT'S RIGHT! YOUR EYES DO NOT DECEIVE YOU!
THE DRAGONZORD AND THE MEGAZORD--ALL SIX RANGERS WORKING TOGETHER! ONCE MORTAL ENEMIES, NOW--DARE I SAY--
SAY IT! SAY IT!
--TEAMMATES?! BUT! HOW WILL THE MASSES RESPOND?!

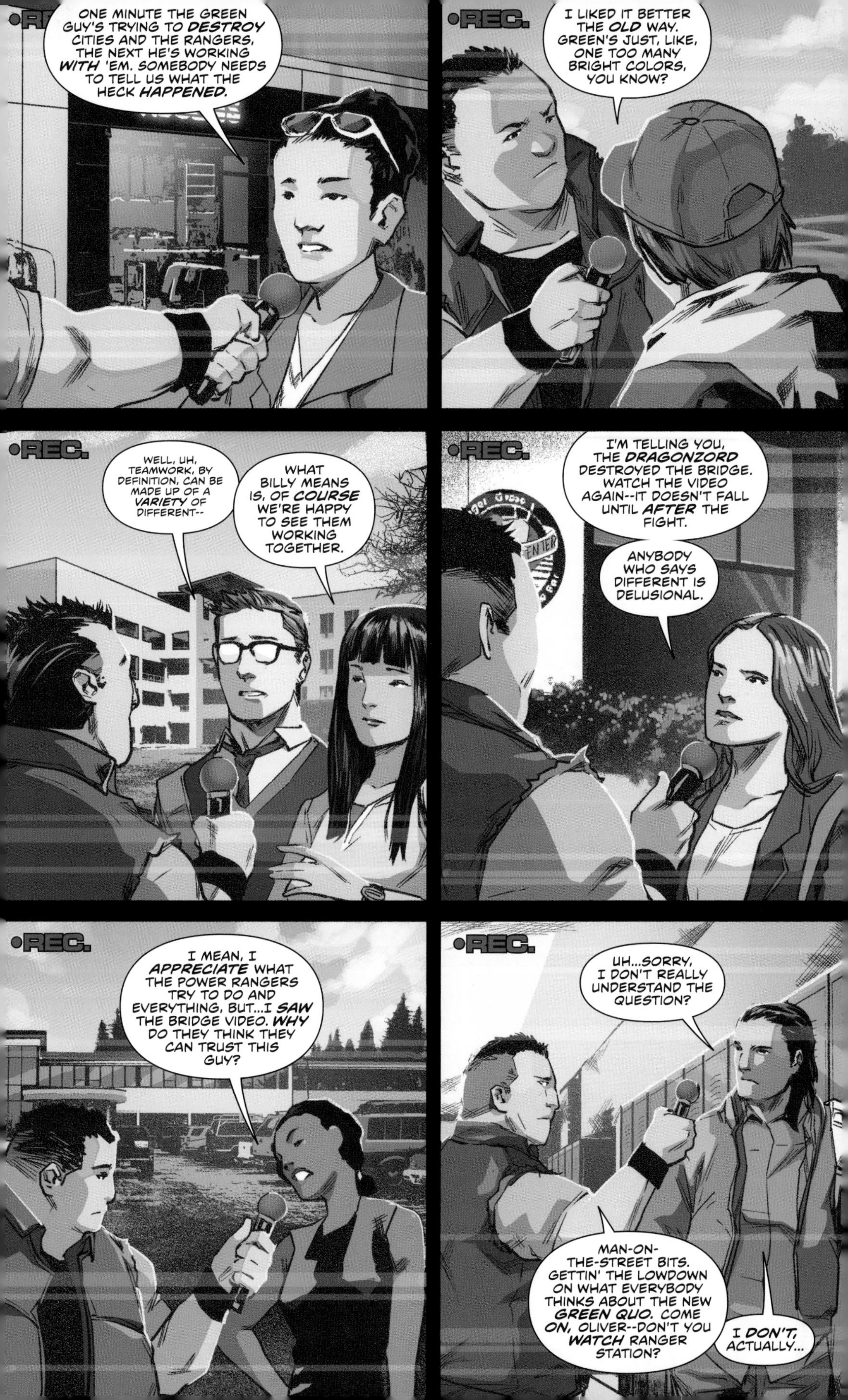

REC.
ONE MINUTE THE GREEN GUY'S TRYING TO DESTROY CITIES AND THE RANGERS, THE NEXT HE'S WORKING WITH 'EM. SOMEBODY NEEDS TO TELL US WHAT THE HECK HAPPENED.
REC.
I LIKED IT BETTER THE OLD WAY. GREEN'S JUST, LIKE, ONE TOO MANY BRIGHT COLORS, YOU KNOW?
REC.
WELL, UH, TEAMWORK, BY DEFINITION, CAN BE MADE UP OF A VARIETY OF DIFFERENT--
WHAT BILLY MEANS IS, OF COURSE WE'RE HAPPY TO SEE THEM WORKING TOGETHER.
REC.
I'M TELLING YOU, THE DRAGONZORD DESTROYED THE BRIDGE. WATCH THE VIDEO AGAIN--IT DOESN'T FALL UNTIL AFTER THE FIGHT.
ANYBODY WHO SAYS DIFFERENT IS DELUSIONAL.
REC.
I MEAN, I APPRECIATE WHAT THE POWER RANGERS TRY TO DO AND EVERYTHING, BUT...I SAW THE BRIDGE VIDEO. WHY DO THEY THINK THEY CAN TRUST THIS GUY?
REC.
UH...SORRY, I DON'T REALLY UNDERSTAND THE QUESTION?
MAN-ON-THE-STREET BITS. GETTIN' THE LOWDOWN ON WHAT EVERYBODY THINKS ABOUT THE NEW GREEN QUO. COME ON, OLIVER--DON'T YOU WATCH RANGER STATION?
I DON'T, ACTUALLY...

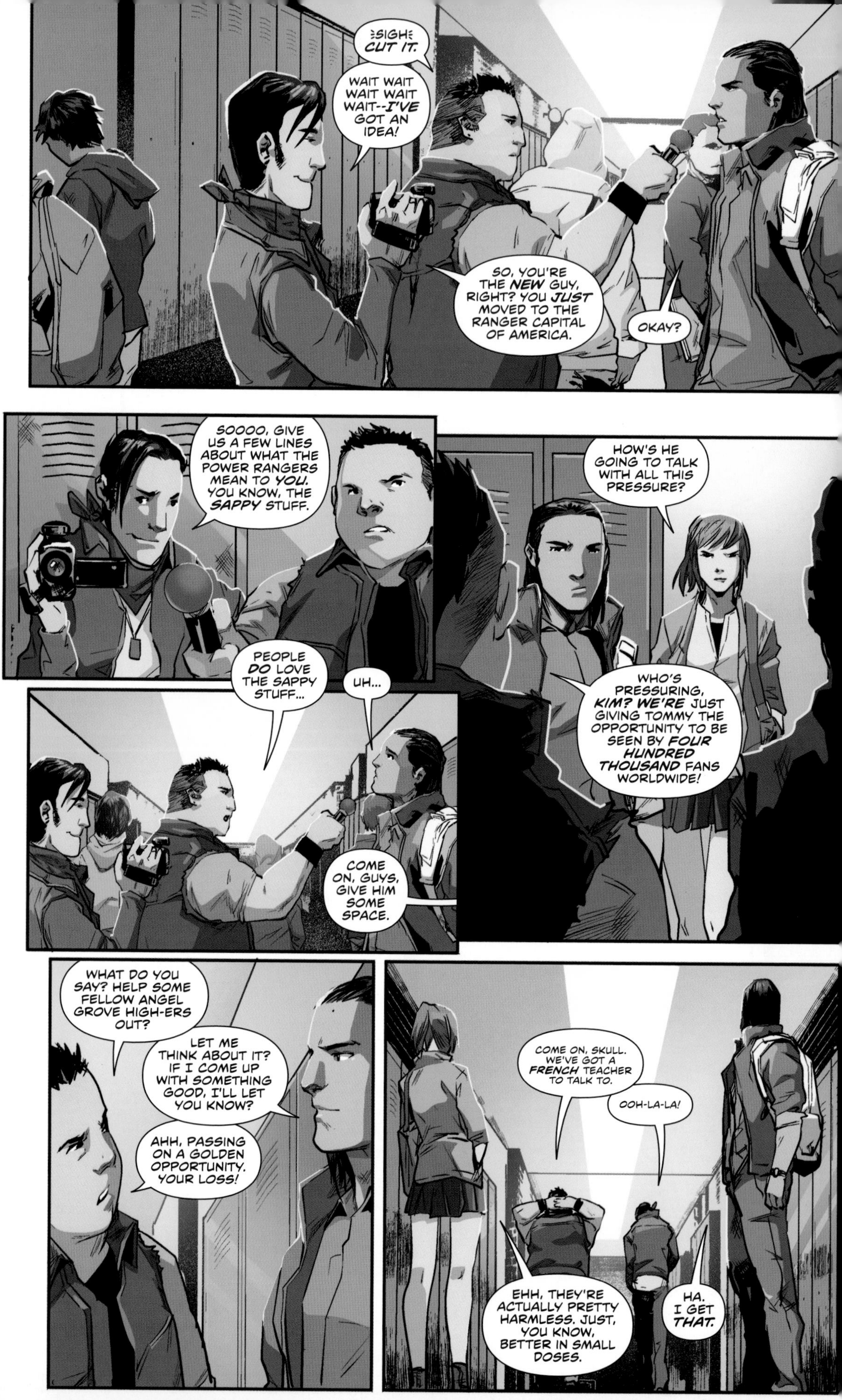
SIGH
CUT IT.
WAIT WAIT WAIT WAIT WAIT--I'VE GOT AN IDEA!
SO, YOU'RE THE NEW GUY, RIGHT? YOU JUST MOVED TO THE RANGER CAPITAL OF AMERICA.
OKAY?
SOOOO, GIVE US A FEW LINES ABOUT WHAT THE POWER RANGERS MEAN TO YOU. YOU KNOW, THE SAPPY STUFF.
HOW'S HE GOING TO TALK WITH ALL THIS PRESSURE?
WHO'S PRESSURING, KIM? WE'RE JUST GIVING TOMMY THE OPPORTUNITY TO BE SEEN BY FOUR HUNDRED THOUSAND FANS WORLDWIDE!
PEOPLE DO LOVE THE SAPPY STUFF...
UH...
COME ON, GUYS, GIVE HIM SOME SPACE.
WHAT DO YOU SAY? HELP SOME FELLOW ANGEL GROVE HIGH-ERS OUT?
LET ME THINK ABOUT IT? IF I COME UP WITH SOMETHING GOOD, I'LL LET YOU KNOW?
AHH, PASSING ON A GOLDEN OPPORTUNITY. YOUR LOSS!
COME ON, SKULL. WE'VE GOT A FRENCH TEACHER TO TALK TO.
OOH-LA-LA!
EHH, THEY'RE ACTUALLY PRETTY HARMLESS. JUST, YOU KNOW, BETTER IN SMALL DOSES.
HA. I GET THAT.

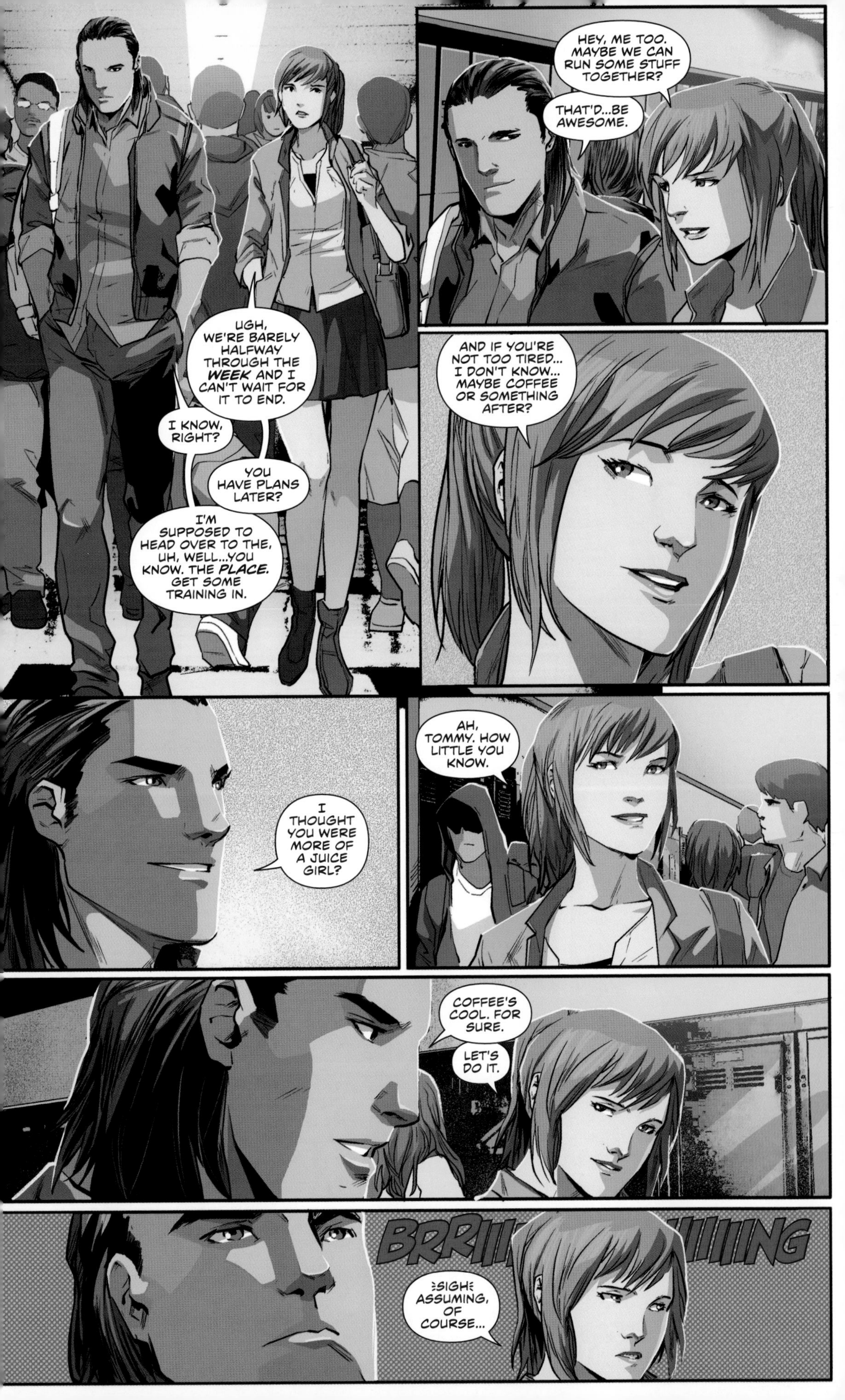
UGH, WE'RE BARELY HALFWAY THROUGH THE *WEEK* AND I CAN'T WAIT FOR IT TO END.
I KNOW, RIGHT?
YOU HAVE PLANS LATER?
I'M SUPPOSED TO HEAD OVER TO THE, UH, WELL...YOU KNOW. THE *PLACE*. GET SOME TRAINING IN.
HEY, ME TOO. MAYBE WE CAN RUN SOME STUFF TOGETHER?
THAT'D...BE AWESOME.
AND IF YOU'RE NOT TOO TIRED... I DON'T KNOW... MAYBE COFFEE OR SOMETHING AFTER?
I THOUGHT YOU WERE MORE OF A JUICE GIRL?
AH, TOMMY. HOW LITTLE YOU KNOW.
COFFEE'S COOL. FOR SURE.
LET'S DO IT.
BRRIII IIIIING
SIGH ASSUMING, OF COURSE...

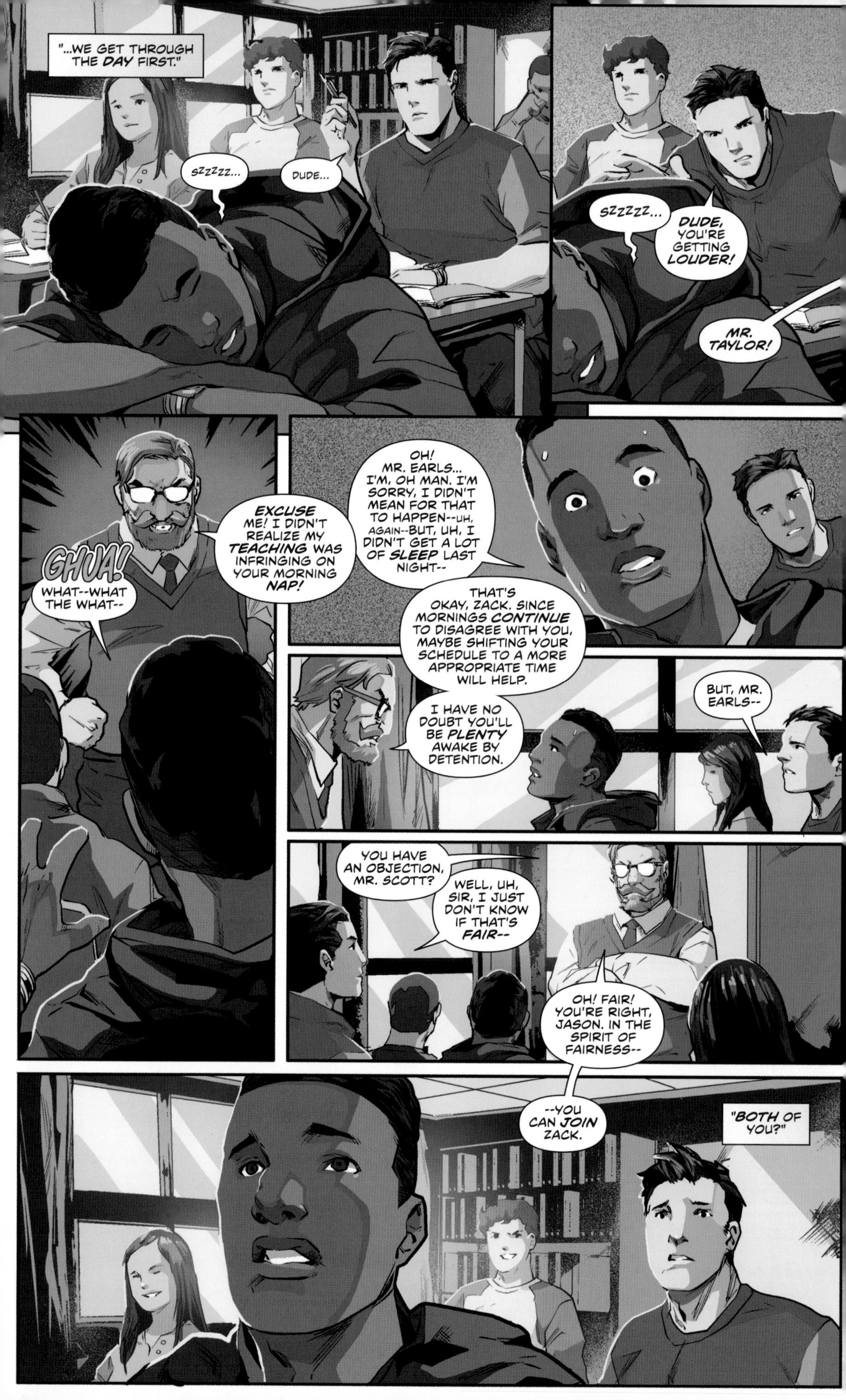
"...WE GET THROUGH THE DAY FIRST."
SZZZZZ...
DUDE...
SZZZZZ...
DUDE, YOU'RE GETTING LOUDER!
MR. TAYLOR!
EXCUSE ME! I DIDN'T REALIZE MY TEACHING WAS INFRINGING ON YOUR MORNING NAP!
GHUA!
WHAT--WHAT THE WHAT--
OH! MR. EARLS... I'M, OH MAN. I'M SORRY, I DIDN'T MEAN FOR THAT TO HAPPEN--UH, AGAIN--BUT, UH, I DIDN'T GET A LOT OF SLEEP LAST NIGHT--
THAT'S OKAY, ZACK. SINCE MORNINGS CONTINUE TO DISAGREE WITH YOU, MAYBE SHIFTING YOUR SCHEDULE TO A MORE APPROPRIATE TIME WILL HELP.
I HAVE NO DOUBT YOU'LL BE PLENTY AWAKE BY DETENTION.
BUT, MR. EARLS--
YOU HAVE AN OBJECTION, MR. SCOTT?
WELL, UH, SIR, I JUST DON'T KNOW IF THAT'S FAIR--
OH! FAIR! YOU'RE RIGHT, JASON. IN THE SPIRIT OF FAIRNESS--
--YOU CAN JOIN ZACK.
"BOTH OF YOU?"

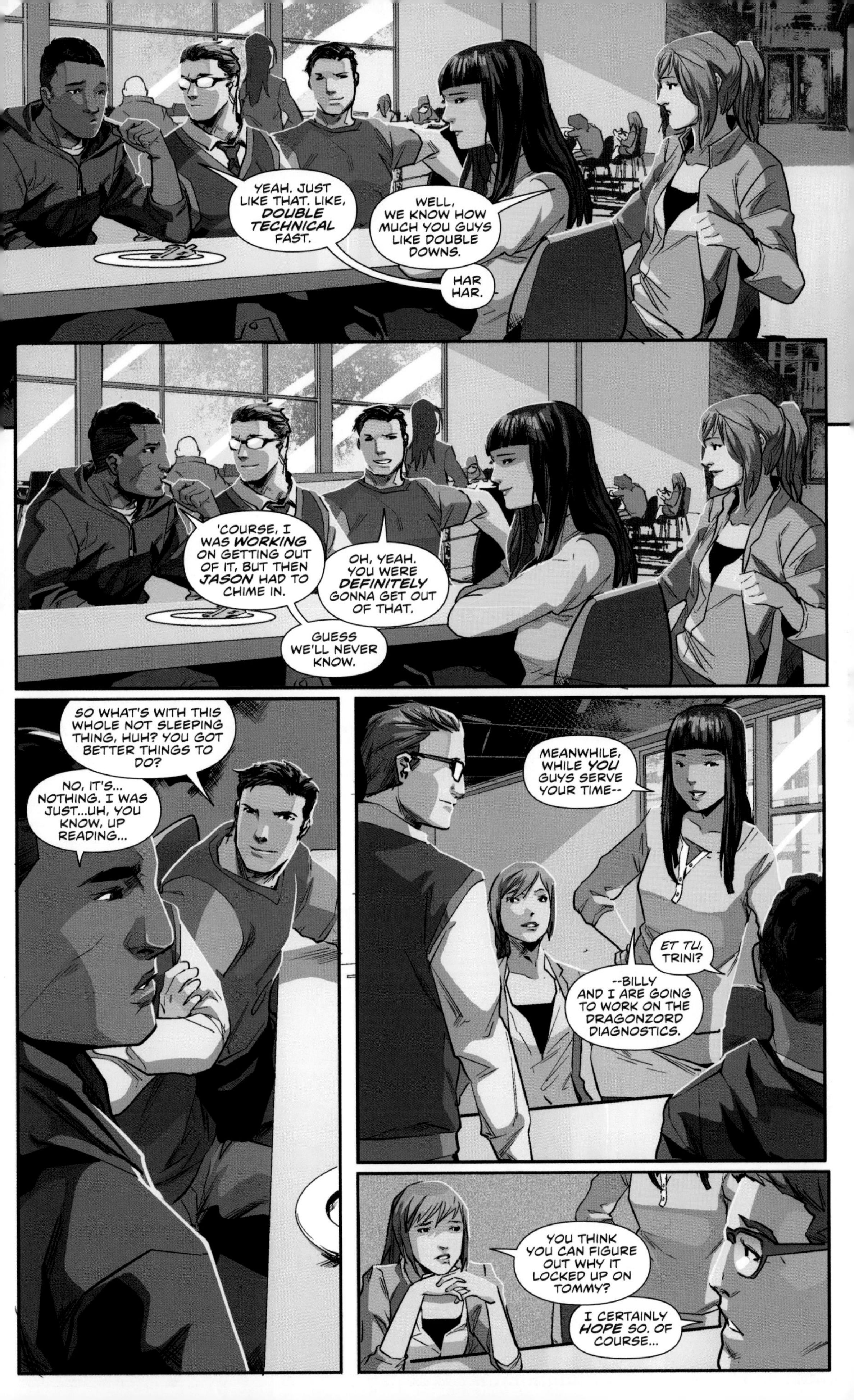
YEAH. JUST LIKE THAT. LIKE, *DOUBLE TECHNICAL* FAST.
WELL, WE KNOW HOW MUCH YOU GUYS LIKE DOUBLE DOWNS.
HAR HAR.
'COURSE, I WAS *WORKING* ON GETTING OUT OF IT, BUT THEN *JASON* HAD TO CHIME IN.
OH, YEAH. YOU WERE *DEFINITELY* GONNA GET OUT OF THAT.
GUESS WE'LL NEVER KNOW.
SO WHAT'S WITH THIS WHOLE NOT SLEEPING THING, HUH? YOU GOT BETTER THINGS TO DO?
NO, IT'S... NOTHING. I WAS JUST...UH, YOU KNOW, UP READING...
MEANWHILE, WHILE *YOU* GUYS SERVE YOUR TIME--
ET TU, TRINI?
--BILLY AND I ARE GOING TO WORK ON THE DRAGONZORD DIAGNOSTICS.
YOU THINK YOU CAN FIGURE OUT WHY IT LOCKED UP ON TOMMY?
I CERTAINLY *HOPE* SO. OF COURSE...

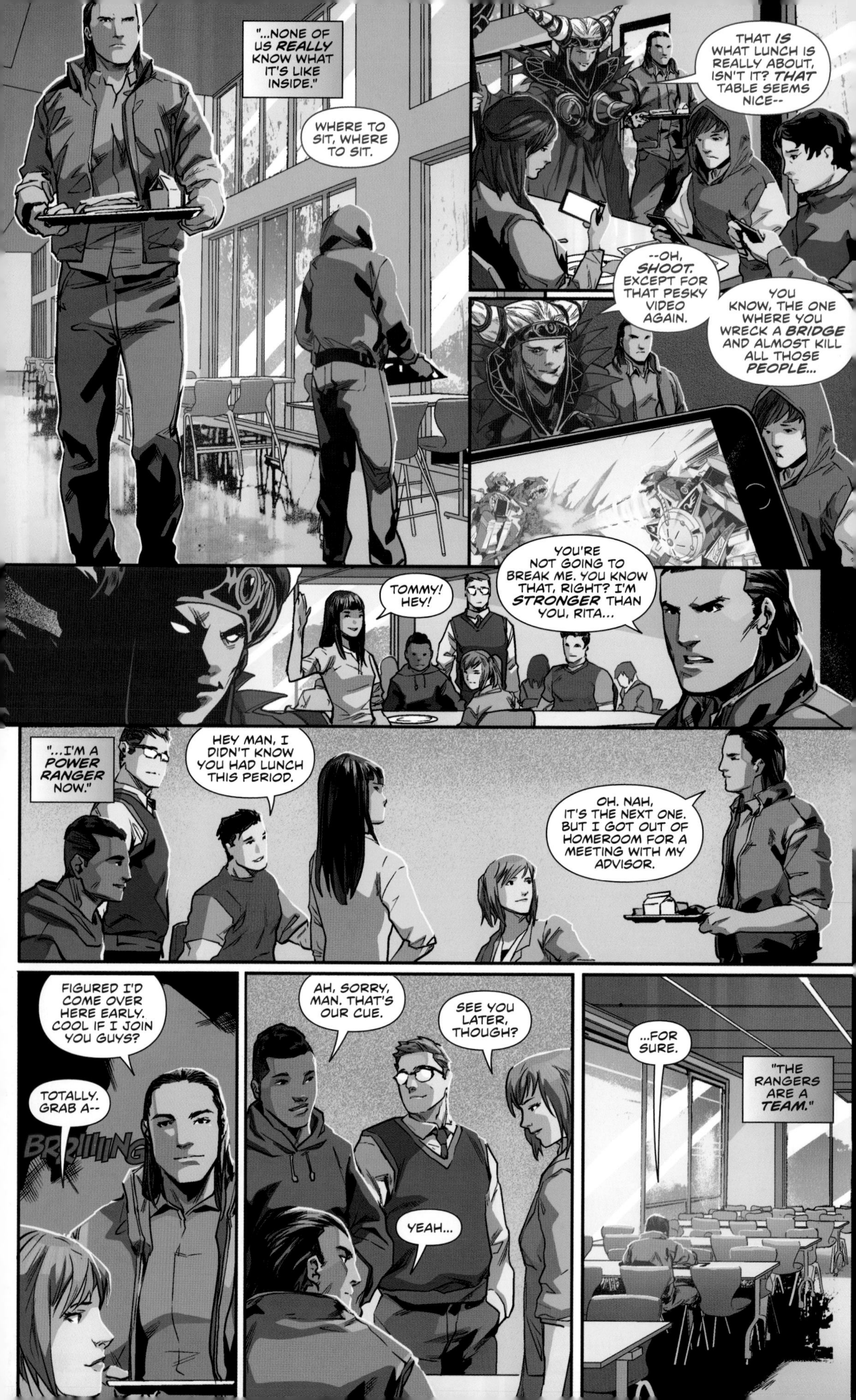
"...NONE OF US REALLY KNOW WHAT IT'S LIKE INSIDE."
WHERE TO SIT, WHERE TO SIT.
THAT IS WHAT LUNCH IS REALLY ABOUT, ISN'T IT? THAT TABLE SEEMS NICE--
--OH, SHOOT. EXCEPT FOR THAT PESKY VIDEO AGAIN.
YOU KNOW, THE ONE WHERE YOU WRECK A BRIDGE AND ALMOST KILL ALL THOSE PEOPLE...
TOMMY! HEY!
YOU'RE NOT GOING TO BREAK ME. YOU KNOW THAT, RIGHT? I'M STRONGER THAN YOU, RITA...
"...I'M A POWER RANGER NOW."
HEY MAN, I DIDN'T KNOW YOU HAD LUNCH THIS PERIOD.
OH. NAH, IT'S THE NEXT ONE. BUT I GOT OUT OF HOMEROOM FOR A MEETING WITH MY ADVISOR.
FIGURED I'D COME OVER HERE EARLY. COOL IF I JOIN YOU GUYS?
TOTALLY. GRAB A--
BRRIIIING
AH, SORRY, MAN. THAT'S OUR CUE.
SEE YOU LATER, THOUGH?
YEAH...
...FOR SURE.
"THE RANGERS ARE A TEAM."

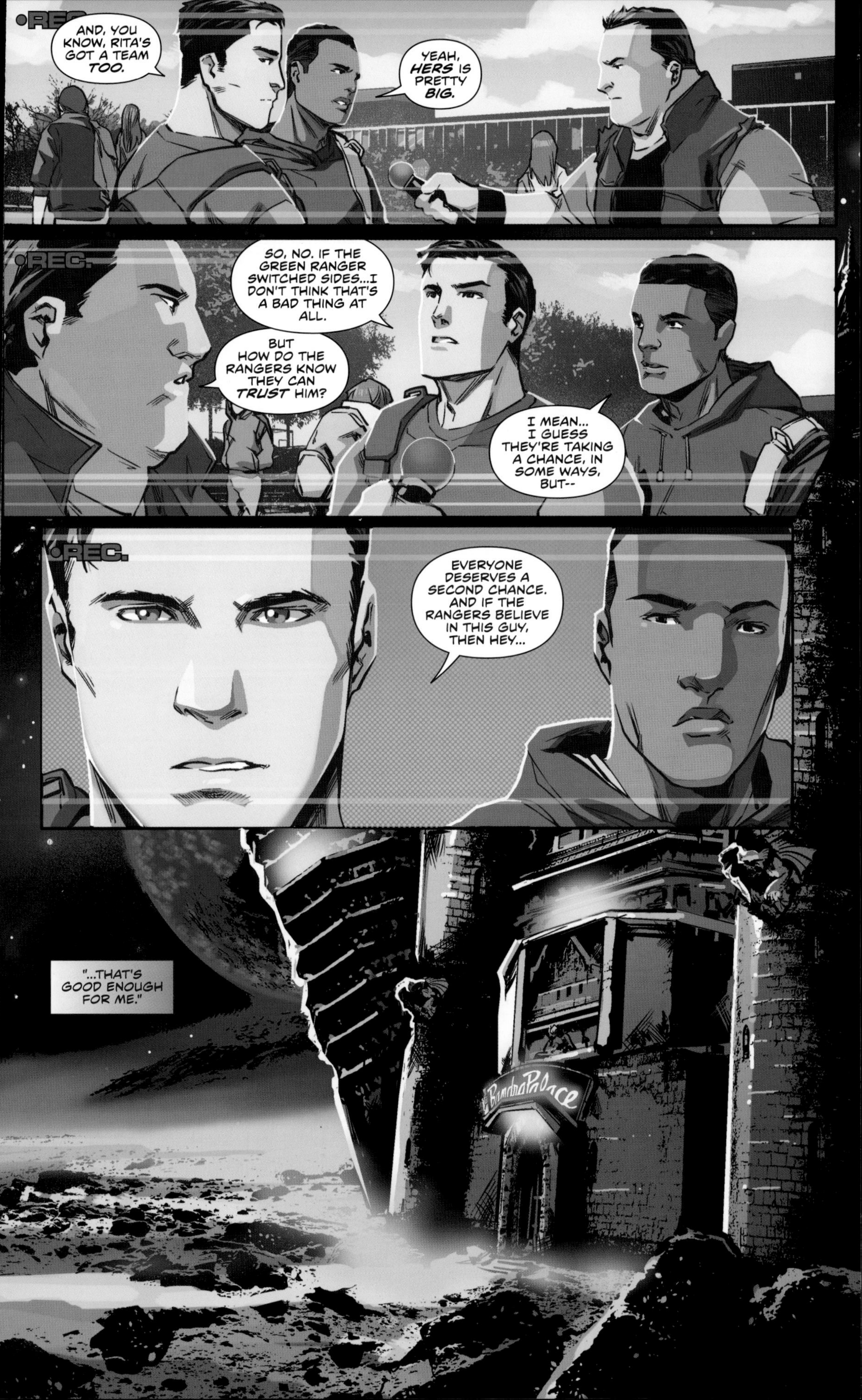

REC.
AND, YOU KNOW, RITA'S GOT A TEAM TOO.
YEAH, HERS IS PRETTY BIG.
REC.
SO, NO. IF THE GREEN RANGER SWITCHED SIDES...I DON'T THINK THAT'S A BAD THING AT ALL.
BUT HOW DO THE RANGERS KNOW THEY CAN TRUST HIM?
I MEAN... I GUESS THEY'RE TAKING A CHANCE, IN SOME WAYS, BUT--
REC.
EVERYONE DESERVES A SECOND CHANCE. AND IF THE RANGERS BELIEVE IN THIS GUY, THEN HEY...
"...THAT'S GOOD ENOUGH FOR ME."
BandoraPalace

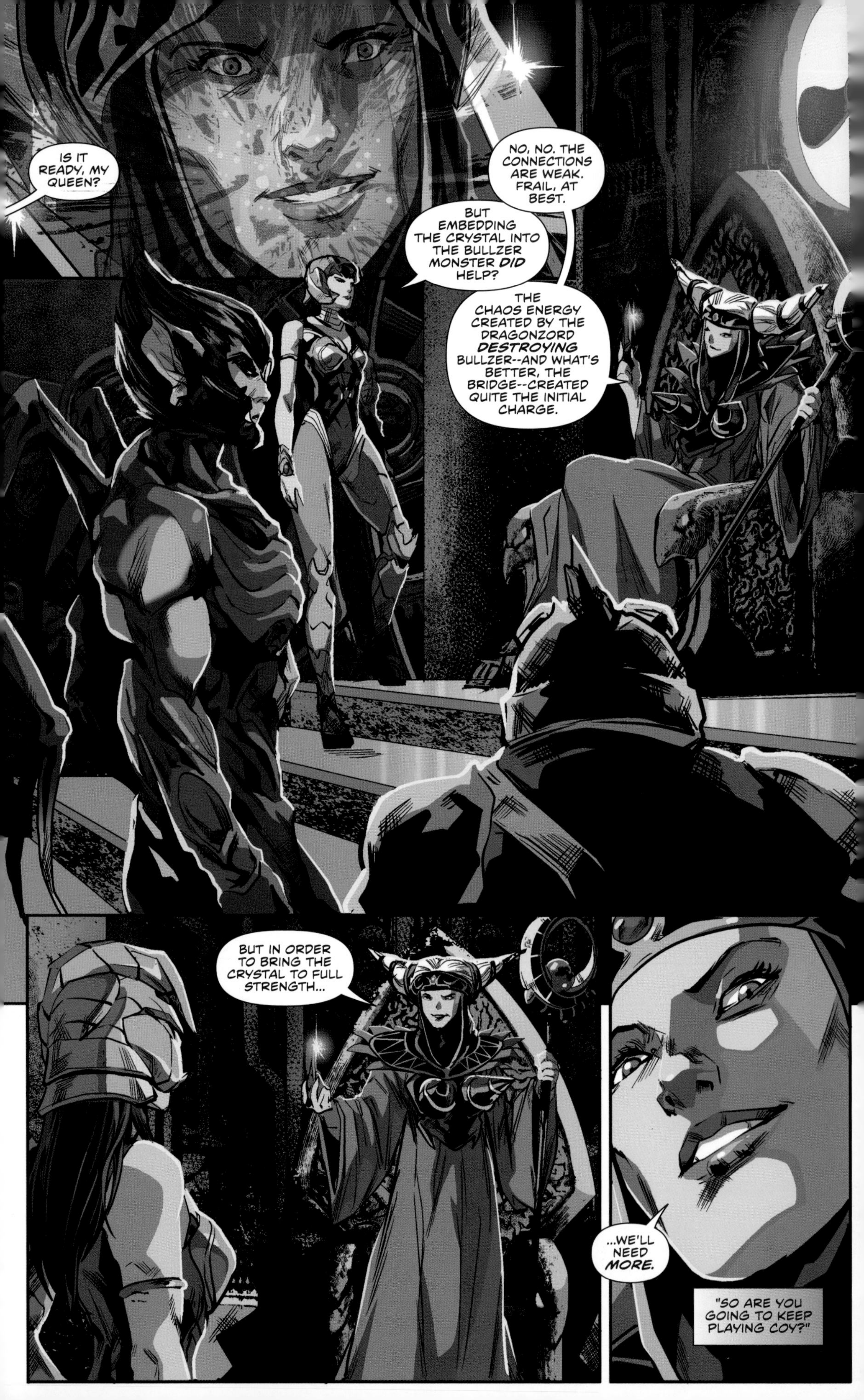
IS IT READY, MY QUEEN?
NO, NO. THE CONNECTIONS ARE WEAK. FRAIL, AT BEST.
BUT EMBEDDING THE CRYSTAL INTO THE BULLZER MONSTER *DID* HELP?
THE CHAOS ENERGY CREATED BY THE DRAGONZORD *DESTROYING* BULLZER--AND WHAT'S BETTER, THE BRIDGE--CREATED QUITE THE INITIAL CHARGE.
BUT IN ORDER TO BRING THE CRYSTAL TO FULL STRENGTH...
...WE'LL NEED *MORE.*
"SO ARE YOU GOING TO KEEP PLAYING COY?"

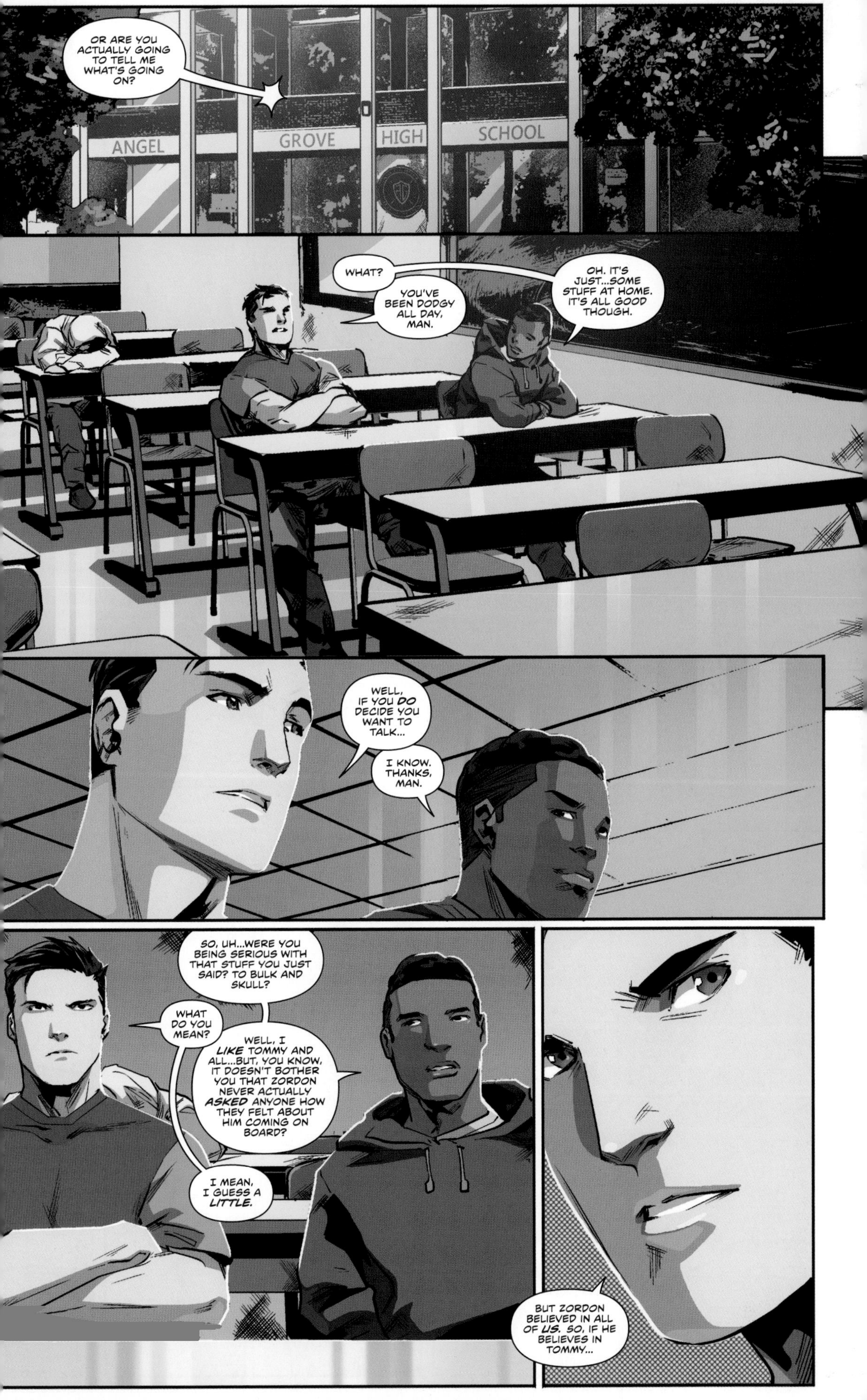
OR ARE YOU ACTUALLY GOING TO TELL ME WHAT'S GOING ON?
ANGEL GROVE HIGH SCHOOL
WHAT?
YOU'VE BEEN DODGY ALL DAY, MAN.
OH. IT'S JUST...SOME STUFF AT HOME. IT'S ALL GOOD THOUGH.
WELL, IF YOU DO DECIDE YOU WANT TO TALK...
I KNOW. THANKS, MAN.
SO, UH...WERE YOU BEING SERIOUS WITH THAT STUFF YOU JUST SAID? TO BULK AND SKULL?
WHAT DO YOU MEAN?
WELL, I LIKE TOMMY AND ALL...BUT, YOU KNOW, IT DOESN'T BOTHER YOU THAT ZORDON NEVER ACTUALLY ASKED ANYONE HOW THEY FELT ABOUT HIM COMING ON BOARD?
I MEAN, I GUESS A LITTLE.
BUT ZORDON BELIEVED IN ALL OF US. SO, IF HE BELIEVES IN TOMMY...

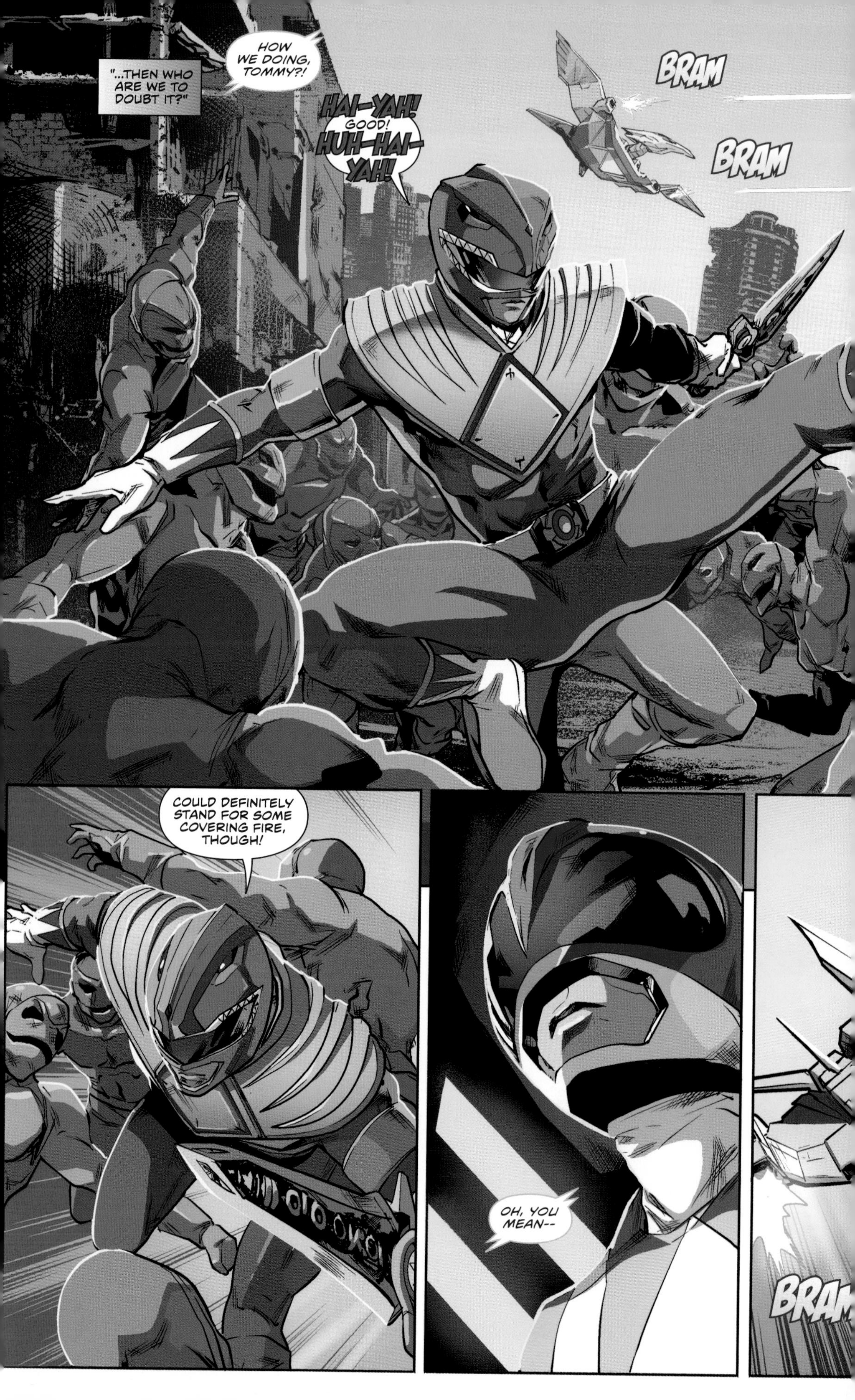
"...THEN WHO ARE WE TO DOUBT IT?"
HOW WE DOING, TOMMY?!
HAI-YAH! GOOD! HUH-HAI-YAH!
BRAM
BRAM
COULD DEFINITELY STAND FOR SOME COVERING FIRE, THOUGH!
OH, YOU MEAN--
BRAM

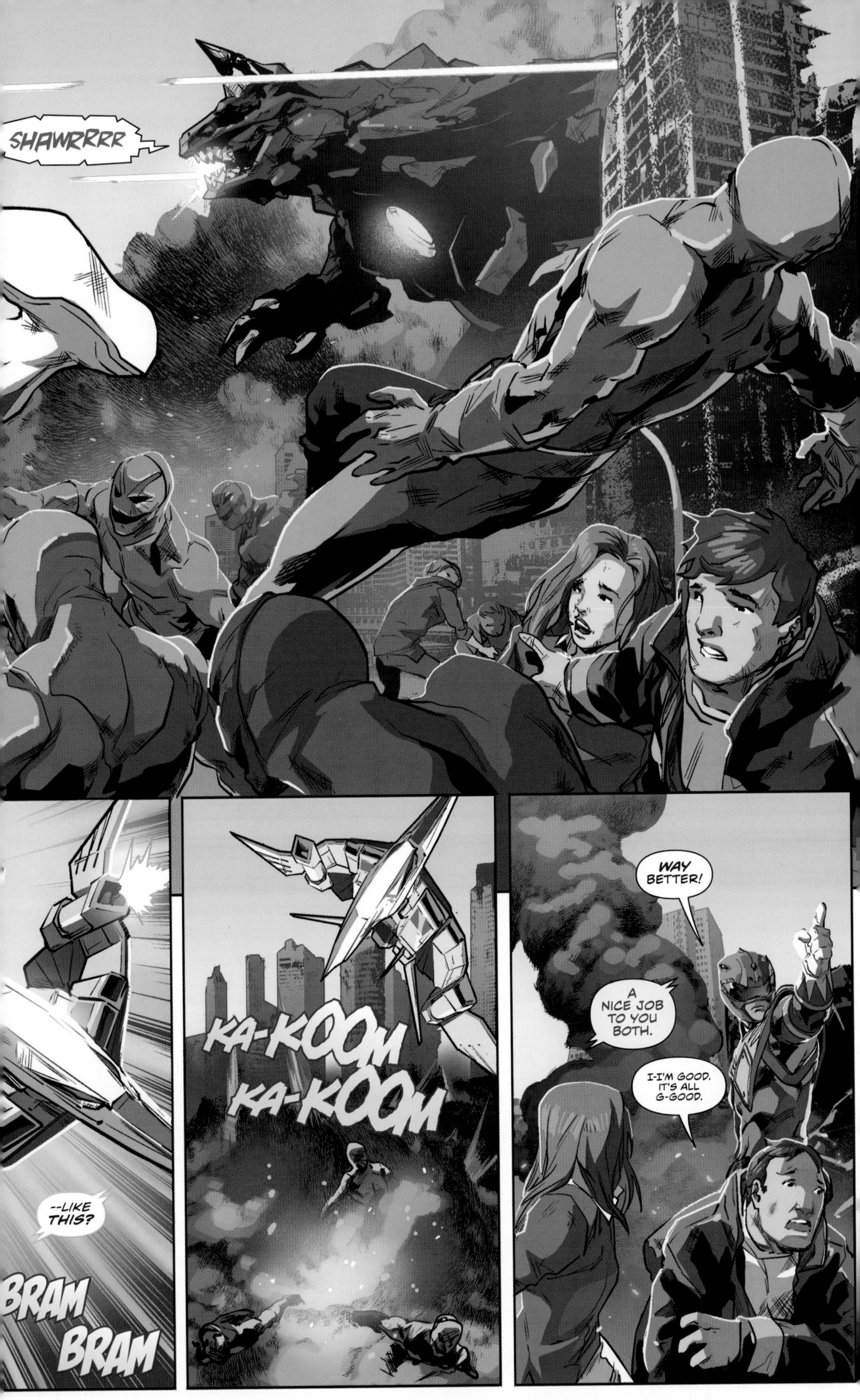
SHAWRRRR
--LIKE THIS?
BRAM
BRAM
KA-KOOM
KA-KOOM
WAY BETTER!
A NICE JOB TO YOU BOTH.
I-I'M GOOD. IT'S ALL G-GOOD.

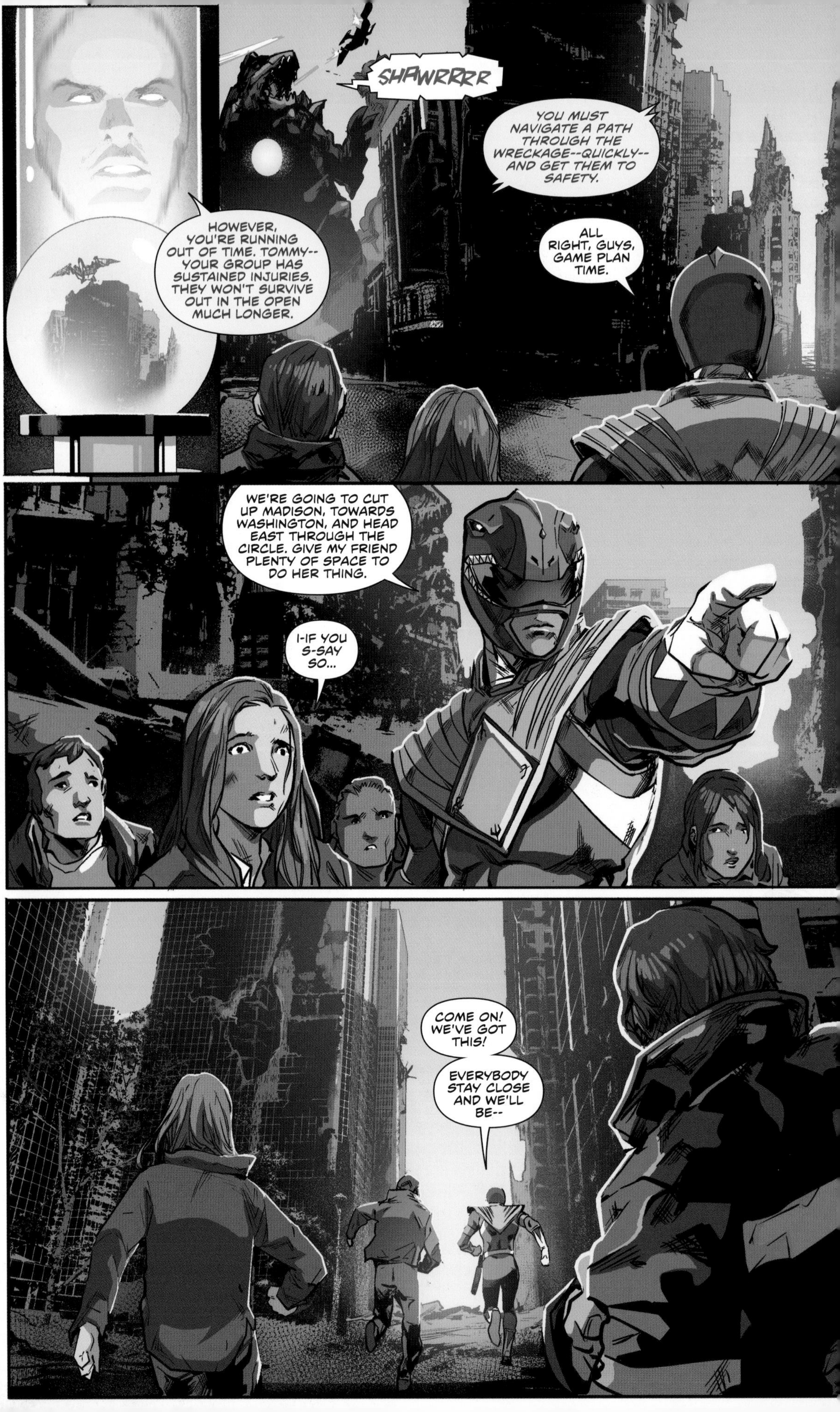
SHAWRRRR
HOWEVER, YOU'RE RUNNING OUT OF TIME. TOMMY-- YOUR GROUP HAS SUSTAINED INJURIES. THEY WON'T SURVIVE OUT IN THE OPEN MUCH LONGER.
YOU MUST NAVIGATE A PATH THROUGH THE WRECKAGE--QUICKLY-- AND GET THEM TO SAFETY.
ALL RIGHT, GUYS, GAME PLAN TIME.
WE'RE GOING TO CUT UP MADISON, TOWARDS WASHINGTON, AND HEAD EAST THROUGH THE CIRCLE. GIVE MY FRIEND PLENTY OF SPACE TO DO HER THING.
I-IF YOU S-SAY SO...
COME ON! WE'VE GOT THIS!
EVERYBODY STAY CLOSE AND WE'LL BE--

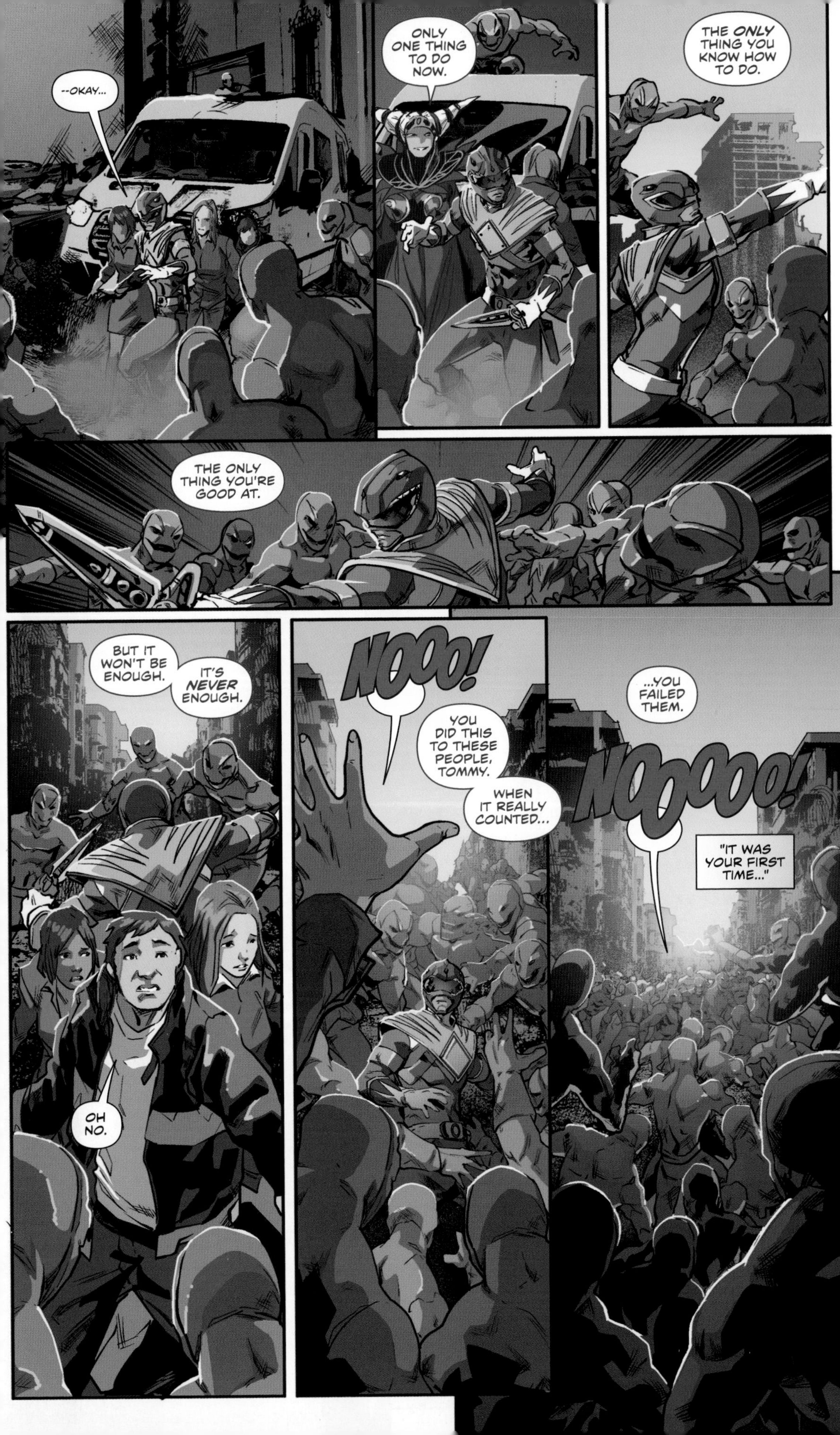
--OKAY...
ONLY ONE THING TO DO NOW.
THE ONLY THING YOU KNOW HOW TO DO.
THE ONLY THING YOU'RE GOOD AT.
BUT IT WON'T BE ENOUGH.
IT'S NEVER ENOUGH.
OH NO.
NOOO!
YOU DID THIS TO THESE PEOPLE, TOMMY.
WHEN IT REALLY COUNTED...
...YOU FAILED THEM.
NOOOOO!
"IT WAS YOUR FIRST TIME..."

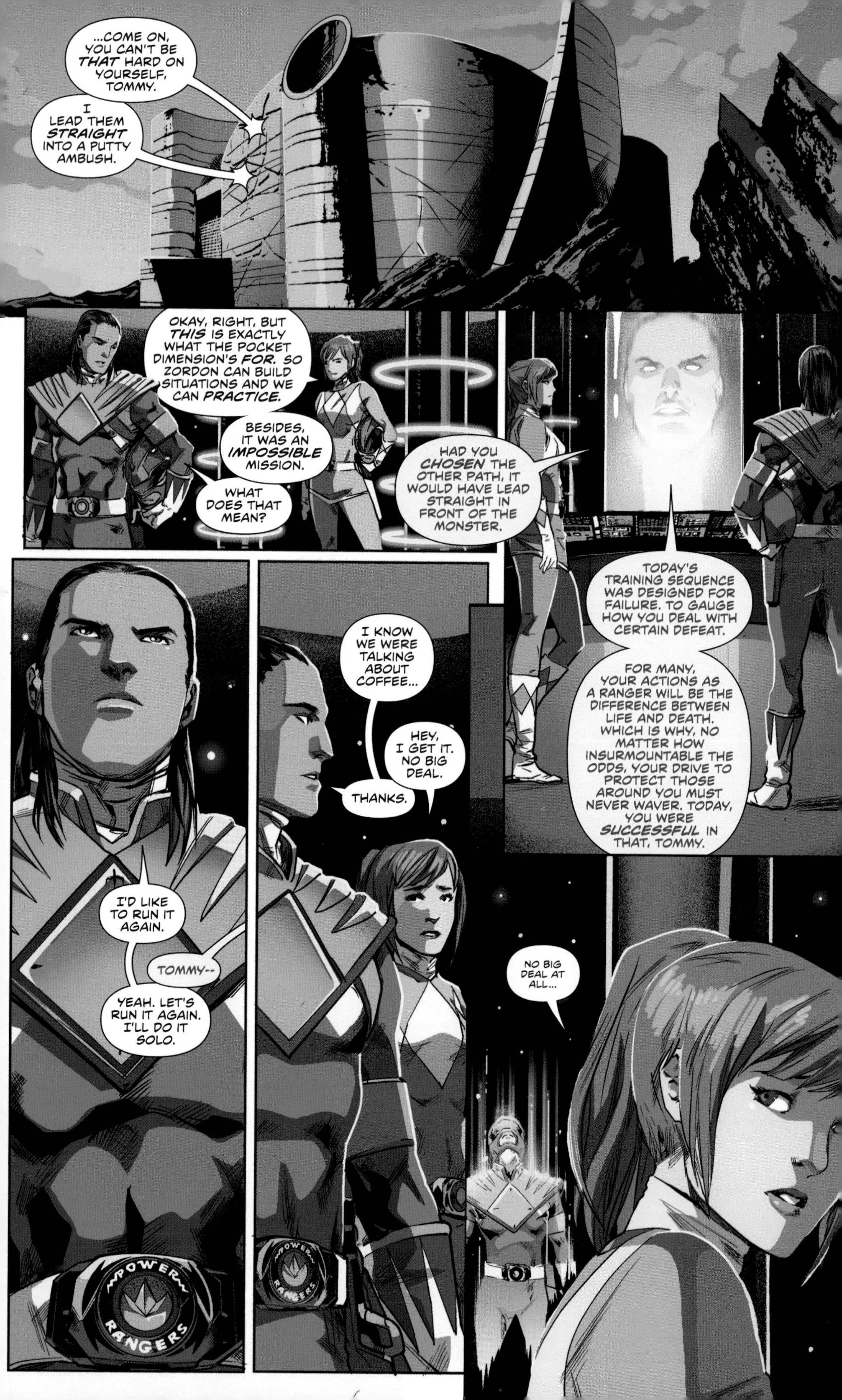

...COME ON, YOU CAN'T BE *THAT* HARD ON YOURSELF, TOMMY.
I LEAD THEM *STRAIGHT* INTO A PUTTY AMBUSH.
OKAY, RIGHT, BUT *THIS* IS EXACTLY WHAT THE POCKET DIMENSION'S *FOR.* SO ZORDON CAN BUILD SITUATIONS AND WE CAN *PRACTICE.*
BESIDES, IT WAS AN *IMPOSSIBLE* MISSION.
WHAT DOES THAT MEAN?
HAD YOU *CHOSEN* THE OTHER PATH, IT WOULD HAVE LEAD STRAIGHT IN FRONT OF THE MONSTER.
TODAY'S TRAINING SEQUENCE WAS DESIGNED FOR FAILURE. TO GAUGE HOW YOU DEAL WITH CERTAIN DEFEAT.
FOR MANY, YOUR ACTIONS AS A RANGER WILL BE THE DIFFERENCE BETWEEN LIFE AND DEATH. WHICH IS WHY, NO MATTER HOW INSURMOUNTABLE THE ODDS, YOUR DRIVE TO PROTECT THOSE AROUND YOU MUST NEVER WAVER. TODAY, YOU WERE *SUCCESSFUL* IN THAT, TOMMY.
I'D LIKE TO RUN IT AGAIN.
TOMMY--
YEAH. LET'S RUN IT AGAIN. I'LL DO IT SOLO.
I KNOW WE WERE TALKING ABOUT COFFEE...
HEY, I GET IT. NO BIG DEAL.
THANKS.
NO BIG DEAL AT ALL...
POWER RANGERS
POWER RANGERS

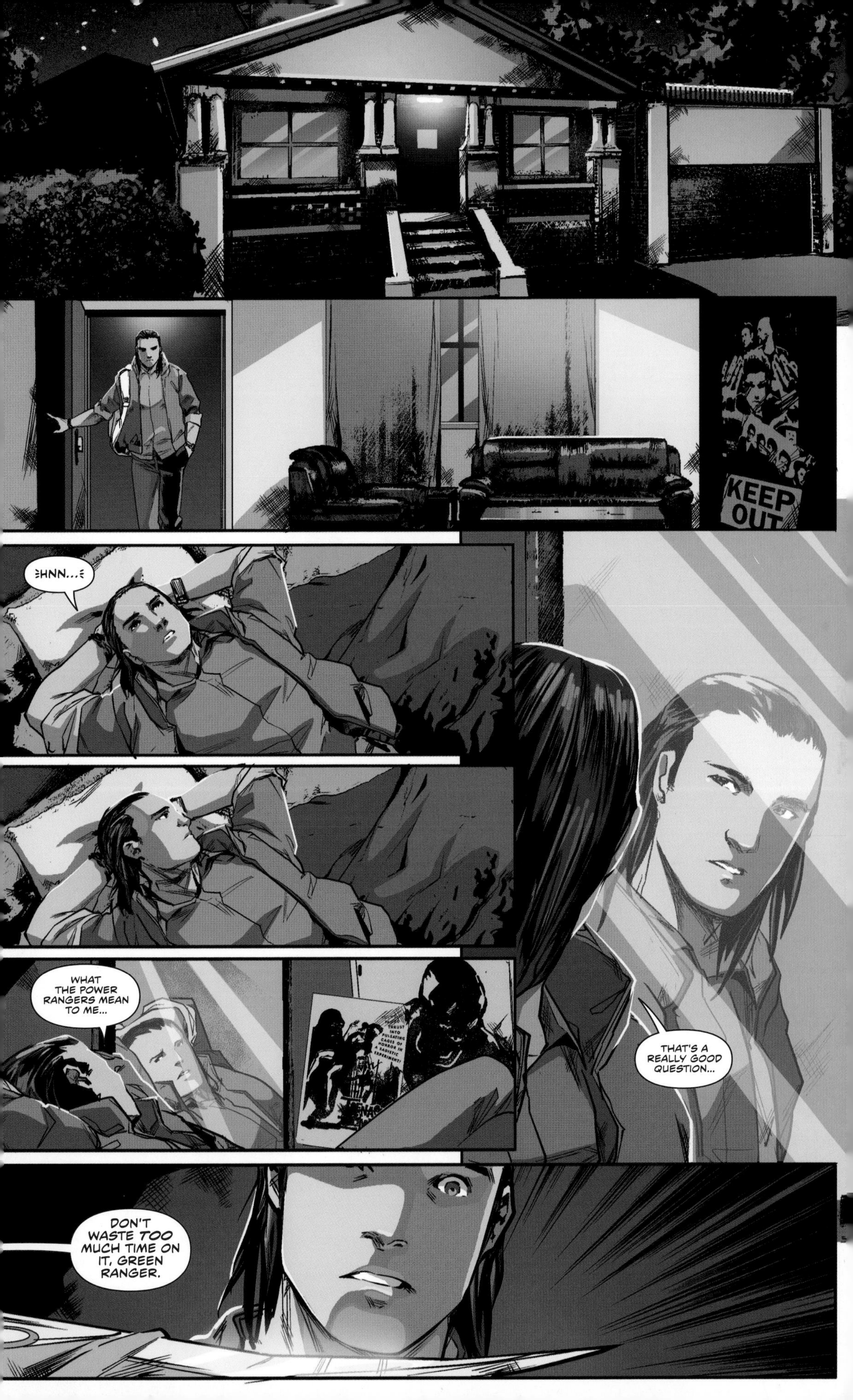
KEEP OUT
HNN...
WHAT THE POWER RANGERS MEAN TO ME...
THAT'S A REALLY GOOD QUESTION...
DON'T WASTE *TOO* MUCH TIME ON IT, GREEN RANGER.

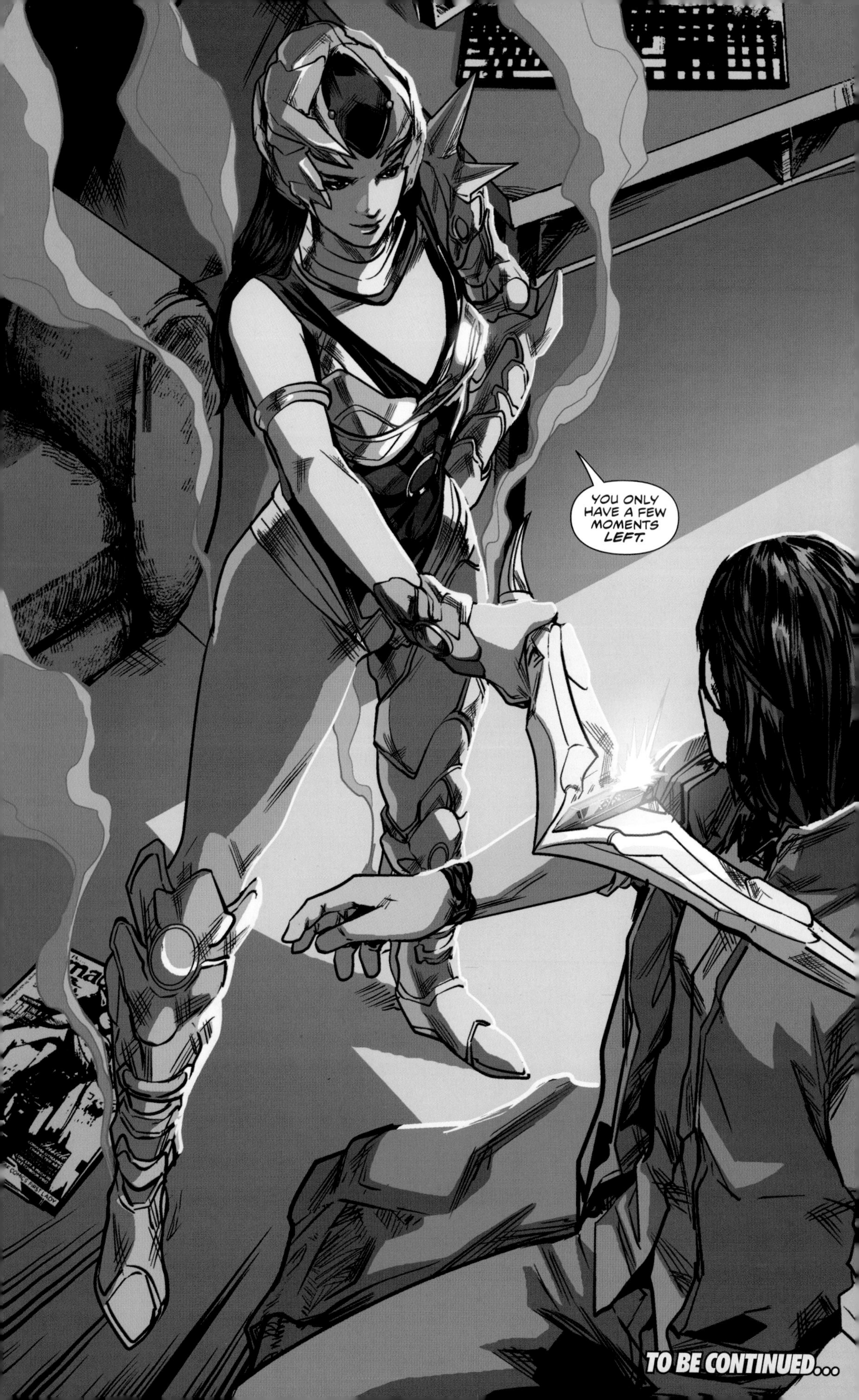
YOU ONLY HAVE A FEW MOMENTS LEFT.
TO BE CONTINUED...

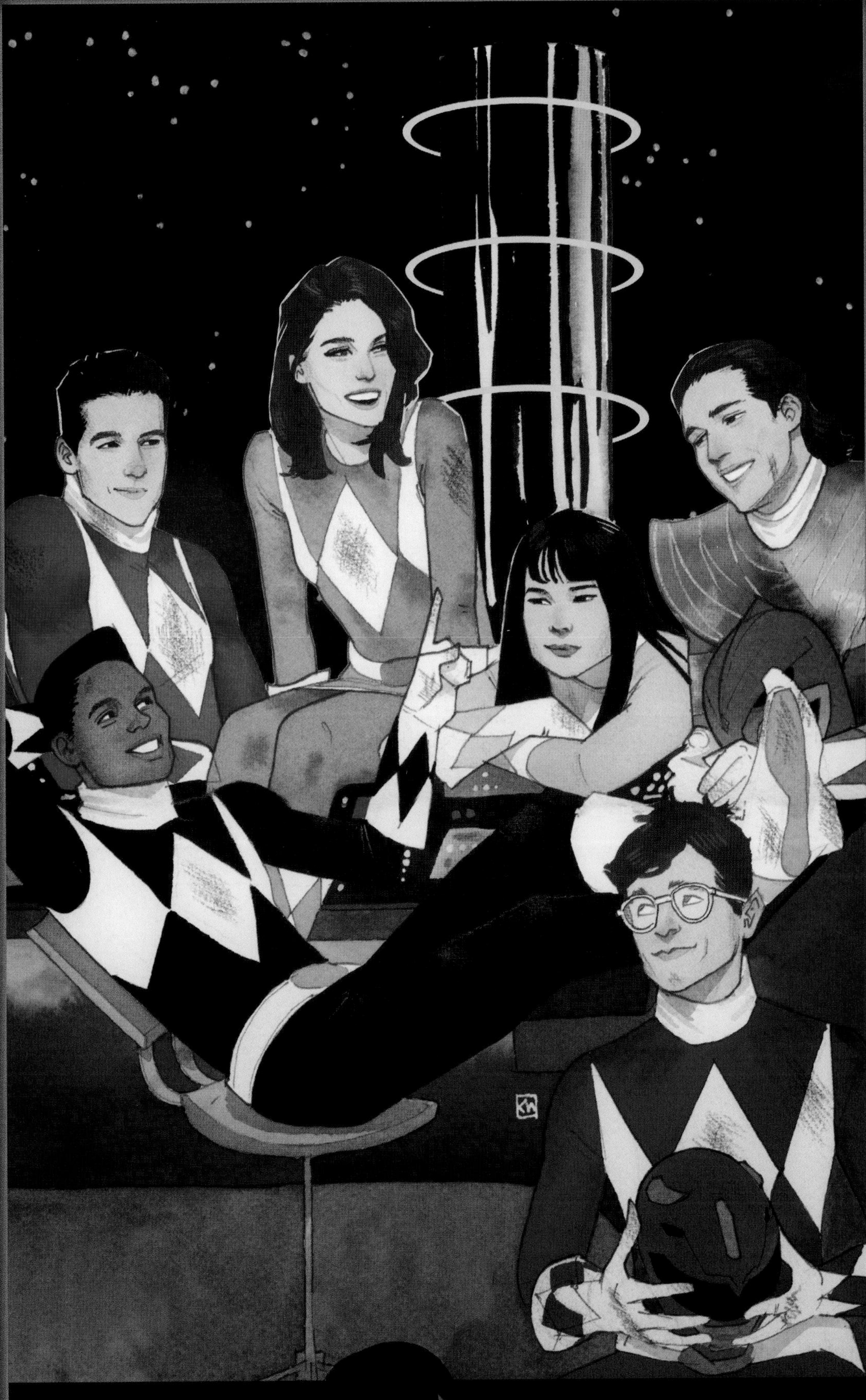

KEVIN WADA VARIANT COVER